Heads Up!

Nancy and Brenda ran to the float. As they climbed up to the haystack, Nancy saw a scarecrow lying on top. It had a huge pumpkin head and mean-looking eyes.

"That scarecrow is ugly," Brenda said. Her voice was shaking.

"Yeah," Nancy agreed. "It would scare me if I were a crow."

Just then the pumpkin head turned slowly. It was looking at them!

"Do you see what I see?" Brenda asked, grabbing Nancy's arm.

Nancy gulped. "I—I think it's, it's—alive."

Nancy and Brenda screamed.

The creepy scarecrow was coming straight toward them!

The Nancy Drew Notebooks

Available from MINSTREL Books

#21

THE NANCY DREW NOTEBOOKS®

PRINCESS ON PARADE

CAROLYN KEENE

Illustrated by Anthony Accardo

A MINSTREL® BOOK

PUBLISHED BY POCKET BOOKS

New York   London   Toronto   Sydney   Tokyo   Singapore

A MINSTREL PAPERBACK *Original*

A Minstrel Book published by
POCKET BOOKS, a division of Simon & Schuster Inc.
1230 Avenue of the Americas, New York, NY 10020

ISBN: 0-671-00815-3

First Minstrel Books printing November 1997

10 9 8 7 6 5 4 3 2

Cover art by Lina Levy

Printed in the U.S.A.

1

Picking a Princess

We're going to have the best float in the whole parade!" Nancy Drew said, tossing a plastic apple into a straw basket.

"My turn," Bess Marvin called out. Bess was Nancy's best friend. She aimed a plastic orange at the basket but missed. Instead of landing inside, the fruit rolled off the edge of the wooden float.

"Whoops!" Nancy giggled.

It was Thursday, after school. The volunteers of Carl Sandburg Elementary School were helping Ms. Frick, the art teacher. They were preparing their float for the River Heights Fall Festival parade on Sunday.

1

The kids had named the float the Pumpkin Patch Dream. Besides Nancy and Bess, Brenda Carlton, Jason Hutchings, and Jennifer Young were part of the third-grade group working on it. Some fourth- and fifth-graders were helping, too.

"I wish George could be here," Nancy told Bess. Georgia Fayne was Bess's cousin and Nancy's other best friend. Everyone called her George. She had broken her arm in a soccer game a few weeks earlier.

"Me, too," Bess said. "But she's getting her new cast put on today. I can't wait to sign it."

Ms. Frick jumped off the float and stepped back to look at it. "The float's looking good, kids. It just needs a few finishing touches."

Nancy liked Ms. Frick. Each day the teacher wore a different pair of cool earrings. That afternoon she had on huge dangling ones shaped like pumpkins.

"Do you think we'll win the prize for best school float?" Bess asked Nancy.

"Sure!" Nancy said. "We have the only float with a real-live Pumpkin Princess."

"And don't forget," Bess added proudly, "my mom is sewing the princess dress."

Jennifer tied a bright orange ribbon around a bunch of wheat. "I wonder who will get to be the princess."

Jason sat up from the pile of hay he was resting on. He was supposed to be building a haystack. "That stupid princess is going to spoil the whole float!" he complained.

Nancy put her hands on her hips. "Can you think of something better?"

"Yes," Jason said. "And when I do, it'll replace that pumpkin *priss* forever!"

"Maybe you should think about finishing your haystack instead," Bess told him.

Jason tossed some hay at Bess and flopped back onto the stack.

"He's just jealous that the star of the float is a girl," Nancy told Bess.

"You're right," Bess said, pulling the hay from her hair. "Everyone wants to be the Pumpkin Princess."

"I don't think I do," Jennifer said slowly.

"Why not?" Nancy asked, surprised.

Jennifer pointed to the tree stump throne in the center of the float. It was on a platform. "I don't like to be up so high," she said. "Besides, what if my nose started to bleed?"

"That would be gross," a voice said.

Nancy turned to see Brenda Carlton standing right behind her.

"Besides," Brenda went on, "the only girl around here who should be princess is me."

Brenda flipped her dark hair over her shoulder. "I have hair like a princess and eyes like a princess . . ."

"And breath like a dragon," Bess muttered. Nancy and Bess giggled.

"Girls! Girls!" Ms. Frick spoke up.

"The most important thing is having the best float we can, right?"

"Yeah," a fourth-grade boy said. "We can't let River Street Elementary win."

Bess nodded. "They're calling their float the Barnyard Brigade. I heard they're going to dress up in animal costumes."

"I'd rather be a Pumpkin Princess than a *Pig* Princess any day," Nancy said.

"Hi, kids." A man with a bushy mustache walked over to the float. He wore a bright red flower on his checkered jacket.

"It's Cheery Charlie!" Jason said.

"Cheery Charlie's my name," the man said proudly. "And costumes are my game!"

The costumes for the kids on the float had been donated by Cheery Charlie's Costume and Joke Shop. Nancy liked the store. It had not only costumes but other neat things like fake wax lips and funny wigs.

"What do you think of our float, Charlie?" Nancy asked.

Charlie put on a pair of eyeglasses. Attached to the frames were fake eyeballs on springs.

"This float is simply eye-popping!" he said, grinning as the eyeballs bounced up and down.

Nancy laughed as Charlie strolled to look at the other side of the float.

"My cousin Tracy is having a costume party for her birthday tomorrow," Jennifer told Nancy. "I looked for a costume in Charlie's shop last week, but I couldn't find anything I really liked."

"That's too bad," Nancy said. "But a costume party is a cool idea. What are you going to wear?"

Jennifer sighed. "Just the same gypsy dress I wore last Halloween. Everyone's seen me in it already, even Tracy."

Brenda made a face. "Last Halloween? I'll bet it smells."

"It does not!" Jennifer said. She lowered her eyes.

6

"That's mean, Brenda," Nancy said.

"Stop being so nosy," Brenda sneered. "This isn't a mystery, *Detective* Drew."

Nancy rolled her eyes. She was very good at solving mysteries. But Brenda was always making fun of her detective work.

"Hey, everybody!" Bess called out. "My mom is here with the princess dress!"

Mrs. Marvin's red minivan pulled up to the float behind the school.

"Princess dress?" Charlie asked with a frown. "What princess dress?"

The kids hopped off the float and ran to Mrs. Marvin.

"Taaa-daaaa!" Mrs. Marvin sang. She held up the dress.

"Ooooh, ahhhh!" All the girls gasped.

Jason pretended to gag. "Blaaaaah!"

The dress was light orange with shimmery gold sequins sewn all over it. Yellow and red leaves circled the waist and the ends of the sleeves. Mrs. Marvin had made an orange velvet cape to wear with the dress.

"It's the most beautiful dress I've ever seen!" Nancy cried.

"It almost matches your hair, Nancy," Jennifer said.

"Really?" Nancy asked. She gently touched her reddish gold hair.

"If all the girls will line up quietly," Ms. Frick announced, "we'll have the drawing for the Pumpkin Princess."

The girls swiftly formed a single line in front of Ms. Frick. Nancy stood behind some fourth-graders. Bess stood behind Nancy, followed by Jennifer.

Everyone watched as Ms. Frick pinned a red number seven onto the dress. She held out a fishbowl filled with small pieces of paper.

"The girl who pulls the lucky seven from the bowl will be the princess," Ms. Frick explained.

Nancy crossed her fingers.

"Good luck, girls," Ms. Frick announced. "I know any one of you will make a great Pumpkin Princess."

Nancy felt someone bump against her back. She spun around and saw Brenda pushing her way in front of Bess.

"Hey," Bess said. "That's not fair!"

"It wouldn't be fair if *you* won," Brenda said. "Your mother made the dress."

Nancy didn't have time to say anything. She was next in line. Reaching into the bowl, Nancy shut her eyes tight.

"Please . . . please . . . please," she whispered, wiggling her fingers through the scraps of paper. She pulled one out. Number nine.

"Oh, well." Nancy sighed and stepped aside.

Brenda dug greedily into the fishbowl. She yanked out a paper and unfolded it.

"Lucky seven!" Brenda squealed. "I won! I'm the Pumpkin Princess!"

Nancy watched Brenda jumping up and down. How could someone so mean be so lucky? she wondered.

"That's mine," Brenda said, grabbing the dress from Mrs. Marvin's hands.

Bess marched over to Brenda. "If you hadn't pushed in front of me, I might have been the Pumpkin Princess!"

"Don't be such a sore loser, Bess." Brenda twirled around with the dress.

"You're the loser, Brenda Carlton!" Bess shouted. She tugged at the dress.

"Let go of it!" Brenda yelled.

"No way!" Bess yelled back, and pulled even harder.

"Bess, Brenda!" Mrs. Marvin shouted.

Ms. Frick ran over, her pumpkin earrings swinging. "Girls! Stop pulling the dress. You're going to—"

RRRRRRRRRRIPPPPPPP!!!

2

Snatched from the Patch

Brenda and Bess dropped the dress.

"I think they tore it," a girl said.

Nancy heard Jason laughing. He was holding up two pieces of heavy paper. It was the paper that had made the ripping sound, not the dress.

"Very sneaky, Jason," Brenda said.

Ms. Frick picked up the dress and shook it out. "It *was* sneaky. But at least he got you girls to stop fighting."

Cheery Charlie marched over to Ms. Frick. "Why didn't you get the Pumpkin Princess dress at my shop along with all the other costumes?" he asked.

"I volunteered to make the dress, Charlie," Mrs. Marvin said.

Charlie shook his head. "But I have a beautiful pumpkin dress in my shop. It's made of chicken wire and foam rubber."

Brenda made a face. "Sounds gross."

Charlie smiled at Brenda. "So this is the lucky Pumpkin Princess."

Brenda flipped her hair. "That's me."

"Well, then, I need the opinion of a beautiful princess." Charlie touched the carnation on his jacket. "Would you tell me how my flower smells?"

"Okay." Brenda leaned in to smell it.

When Brenda was close, water gushed from Charlie's red flower and squirted her right in the face!

"Bleeeech!" Brenda sputtered.

All the kids laughed. Even Mrs. Marvin and Ms. Frick smiled.

"Serves her right," Bess said.

"We all want to use Mrs. Marvin's dress in the parade," Ms. Frick told Charlie when everyone had quieted down.

Charlie took a deep breath. "Suit yourself. But I'm not happy about this." He turned on his heel and walked away.

"Okay, kids," Ms. Frick called out. "When I tell you your parts on the float, I don't want to hear any arguments.

"The fourth- and fifth-graders will wear the apple tree costumes," Ms. Frick announced. "They'll dance along the sides of the float in the parade, just the way we've practiced.

"Jason, you will be the princess's Scarecrow Guard," she continued.

"Crows of the world, watch out!" Jason did a swift karate kick.

"The girls in the third grade will be the princess's Veggies-in-Waiting," Ms. Frick went on.

"Great. Now we have to wait on Princess Snooty!" Bess grumbled to Nancy.

"Nancy will be an ear of corn," Ms. Frick continued, "Jennifer a pea pod, and Bess a stalk of broccoli."

"But, Ms. Frick," Bess wailed, "I hate broccoli!"

"You have to *wear* it, Bess, not eat it," Ms. Frick said.

"Where are our costumes, Ms. Frick?" Jennifer asked.

"The costumes are hanging on a rack in the gym," Ms. Frick explained. She led the kids inside. "I'll hand them out. Then you can try them on."

Nancy climbed into a soft yellow-and-green corn-on-the-cob costume. She peeked out of the hole for her face and giggled.

Once all of the colorful costumes were on, everyone laughed, even Bess. The kids ran outside and chased one another around the float.

Jason sneaked up behind Nancy. He yanked at the back of her corn costume.

"Veggie-wedgie! Veggie-wedgie!" Jason chanted. Nancy was about to push him away when she heard Jennifer scream.

"Jennifer, what is it?" Nancy asked.

Jennifer pointed to a clump of bushes. "Look, over there!" she shouted.

Nancy gasped. A pair of moose antlers, a bright red rooster comb, and two pig ears were bobbing above the bushes.

"Those aren't real animals," Brenda said. She marched over to the bushes and spread them apart. "See? They're just kids in dumb costumes."

Three boys dressed as animals stepped out from behind the bushes.

"They must be from River Street Elementary School," Nancy said to Bess. "And they're spying on us."

The boy in the pig costume pointed at Nancy. "That's the *corniest* costume I've ever seen!"

Then Ms. Frick walked over. "Well, it looks as though we have visitors," she said.

The River Street spies took one look at Ms. Frick and began to run away.

"What's the matter?" Jason yelled. "You chicken?"

"No way," one of the River Street kids called over his shoulder. "I'm a rooster!"

Then the boys ran off.

"Those costumes were dopey," a fourth-grade boy said.

"Our float will be much better," Jennifer said.

"Okay, everyone," Ms. Frick called out. "It's time to hang up your costumes."

Brenda raised her hand. "Ms. Frick, may I take my costume home? Please?"

Ms. Frick shook her head. "No costume is to leave the school."

Brenda stuck out her lower lip. "But I'm the princess!"

"And I'm the *teacher*," Ms. Frick said with a firm smile. "Go inside and hang up your costume."

Once the costumes were put away, everyone hurried back outside to the float.

While Nancy put the last of the fruit in her basket, she spotted Brenda carrying a plastic bag under her arm.

Brenda looks like she's doing something sneaky, Nancy thought. I wonder what's inside the bag?

Then Bess tapped Nancy's shoulder. "Nancy, George is here with her new cast!"

"Let's sign it," Nancy said.

Brenda dropped her bag on the float and followed Nancy. "I'm going to sign her cast *Princess* Brenda," she said to Nancy.

"Did it hurt?" a fourth-grade boy asked when everyone was around George.

"It did when I broke it," George admitted. "Now it just itches."

All the kids wanted to sign the new cast, but Ms. Frick was the first. She drew a pretty butterfly with colored pens.

"My turn!" Jason shouted. He took out a pen and scribbled, "Way to go, KLUTZ!"

"What a pain," George groaned as Jason ran back to the float.

The last ones to sign the cast were

Nancy and Bess. Using purple and pink pens, they wrote, "Friends Till the End."

Ms. Frick clapped her hands for attention. "The float is just about finished!" she announced.

The volunteers cheered loudly.

"But don't forget to meet here Saturday afternoon for the big dress rehearsal," Ms. Frick added.

George sighed. "I wish I could be a part of the parade."

"You will," Nancy said. "You're going to cheer for us."

Nancy, Bess, and George took one last look at the float before they went home. Jason was finally throwing hay into a big pile for the haystack.

"It's about time!" Nancy said.

That night at dinner, Nancy laughed as Hannah Gruen placed some food on the table. Hannah was the Drew family's housekeeper.

"You made corn on the cob," Nancy said. "Just like my costume!"

Hannah smiled. "I'll save some for your father. He's working late tonight."

Nancy was about to bite into her corn when the phone rang.

"I'll get it, Hannah," Nancy said. "Maybe it's Daddy."

But it wasn't Mr. Drew. It was Brenda.

"Listen. I'm only going to say it once," Brenda said. "I need you to solve a mystery."

Why would Brenda ask her for help? Nancy wondered. Brenda was always saying that she could solve mysteries better than Nancy.

"What kind of mystery?" Nancy asked.

"The Pumpkin Princess dress," Brenda whispered. "It's been stolen!"

3

A Pinkie Promise

hat do you mean the dress was stolen?" Nancy asked.

"I can't explain now," Brenda said. "Meet me tomorrow morning in the schoolyard. And come alone!"

"But—"

Click!

"Hello? Brenda?"

Nancy heard the dial tone. Brenda had hung up.

"I'll bet there are more names on my cast than on the Declaration of Independence!" George told Nancy and Bess at the playground the next morning.

Just then Nancy spotted Brenda walking toward the swings.

"I've got to go," Nancy said. "I just thought of something I have to do."

"What?" Bess asked.

Nancy bit her lip. She had promised to meet Brenda alone.

"Uh, nothing important," Nancy said. "I'll be right back." She could feel Bess and George watching her as she walked away.

"I thought you'd never leave those two," Brenda said when Nancy sat down on an empty swing.

"Tell me about the dress," Nancy said. "Did you take it home?"

"No way, José!" Brenda said.

"Then what was in that plastic bag I saw you with yesterday?" Nancy asked.

Brenda stared at the ground. "What bag?" she asked.

"I saw it, Brenda." Nancy narrowed her eyes. "You don't really have a mystery, do you?"

"I do!" Brenda said.

"Then tell the truth!" Nancy insisted.

"Okay, okay." Brenda looked away from Nancy. "I was *thinking* of taking the dress and the cape home, so I sneaked them into the bag," she admitted. "I put the bag down when I went to sign George's cast. When I came back, the bag was gone."

Brenda continued. "It's not like I wanted to steal the dress. I just wanted my parents to see how pretty I looked."

"Why didn't you tell Ms. Frick right away?" Nancy asked.

Brenda's eyes opened wide. "I couldn't tell her I was trying to take the dress home. Especially now that it's missing."

The swing creaked as Nancy began to rock back and forth.

"Well? Will you help me find the dress or not?" Brenda demanded.

"Why should I?" Nancy asked.

"If you help me solve this mystery," Brenda said slowly, "I promise to write in my newspaper that Nancy Drew is the greatest detective in the whole world."

Nancy stopped swinging. "The greatest detective in the whole world?" she repeated.

"Front page," Brenda added. "Think of it, Nancy. Everyone reads the *Carlton News*. You'll be famous!"

Nancy didn't care much about being famous. But she would like Brenda to admit in print that she was a good detective.

"I'll do it," Nancy said with a sigh.

"Great, but you have to promise me one thing," Brenda said seriously. "You can't tell anyone about the missing dress. Not your father. Not your housekeeper. And most of all, not Bess and George."

Nancy glanced over at her two best friends. They were still watching her.

"I never keep secrets from Bess and George," Nancy said. Then she thought for a minute. "But the princess dress is important.

"Okay," Nancy said. She hooked her little finger with Brenda's and made a pinkie promise.

"You won't be sorry, Nancy," Brenda said.

Nancy wasn't so sure. From the corner of her eye, she saw Bess and George march away in a huff.

Nancy pulled out a shiny blue notebook from her knapsack. Her father had given it to her for solving mysteries. She turned to a fresh page and wrote: "The Pumpkin Princess Mystery."

"What are you doing?" Brenda asked.

"I'm going to make a list of suspects," Nancy answered.

Brenda jabbed at the page. "Good. Write down the girls who wanted to be the Pumpkin Princess," she ordered.

"Brenda, *all* the girls wanted to be the princess," Nancy said.

"Then put down Bess's name," Brenda said. "She was mad at me and wanted to wear the dress more than anyone."

"Bess couldn't have taken the dress," Nancy said. "She was with me the whole time."

Nancy thought for a minute. Then she wrote down Cheery Charlie's name.

"Charlie was angry that the princess dress didn't come from his shop," Nancy explained. "He might have taken the dress to get even."

"What about the spies from River Street Elementary?" Brenda asked. "They might have sneaked back while everyone was busy signing George's cast."

"Good thinking, Brenda," Nancy said. She added the Barnyard Brigade to her list of suspects.

"This mystery business is a piece of cake," Brenda said.

Nancy shook her head. "Not always. Sometimes it's like finding a needle in a haystack," she said. Then her eyes lit up. The haystack made her think of Jason Hutchings.

"Jason never wanted the Pumpkin Princess in the parade," Nancy thought out loud. "He was also the first to return to the float after signing George's cast."

"So?" Brenda asked.

"He was working on the haystack when everyone was leaving," Nancy said. "Maybe he buried the dress underneath. Come on, let's check it out before school starts!"

Nancy and Brenda hopped off the swings and ran to the float.

As they climbed up to the haystack, Nancy saw a scarecrow lying on top. It had a huge orange pumpkin head made out of papier-mâché and mean-looking eyes.

"That scarecrow is ugly," Brenda said. Her voice was shaking.

"Yeah," Nancy agreed. "It would scare me if I were a crow."

Just then the pumpkin head turned slowly. It was looking at them!

"Do you see what I see?" Brenda asked, grabbing Nancy's arm.

Nancy gulped when she heard the scarecrow growl. "I—I think it's, it's— alive."

Nancy and Brenda screamed.

The creepy scarecrow was coming straight toward them!

4

The Bess Mess

Nancy and Brenda jumped off the float.

"Leave us alone, you ugly pumpkin-headed beast!" Nancy ordered, beginning to run.

The scarecrow leaped down and reached out to grab the girls. He laughed an evil laugh.

"Wait a minute." Nancy turned to face the scarecrow and grabbed the pumpkin head with both hands. "I know that laugh."

She yanked the mask off. "Just as I thought," Nancy said. The scarecrow was Jason Hutchings!

Jason laughed again. "You dared me

to come up with a better idea to replace the Pumpkin Princess."

Nancy and Brenda exchanged glances.

Jason struck a karate stance. "I'm the super pumped-up Power Pumpkin!"

Jason climbed to the top of the haystack and began to rap:

"I'm a pumped-up Power Pumpkin machine,
My talk is tough and my walk is mean,
I'm king of the patch,
And that's the way it should be,
That princess priss is history!"

"What do you think?" Jason asked when he had finished. He jumped down from the haystack.

"I think you hid something under that haystack," Brenda yelled. "That's what I think!"

Jason smiled slyly. "There's only one way to find out," he said. "Take it apart and see for yourself."

Nancy stared at the towering haystack. "No way," she said.

"Why not?" Brenda asked.

"Jason probably didn't hide the dress there," Nancy whispered. "Or else he wouldn't dare us to go through it."

"I'm taking that haystack apart, whether you like it or not!" Brenda said. She climbed onto the float.

"This is going to be good." Jason snickered.

"Brenda, don't," Nancy pleaded.

But Brenda was already tearing through the haystack, making a big mess.

Soon the hay was scattered all over the float. There was no Pumpkin Princess dress anywhere.

"What is going on here?" a voice demanded.

Nancy looked up. Ms. Frick was standing over them, frowning.

"Hello, Ms. Frick," Nancy said shakily. "We were just, um, working."

"Ms. Frick, they took apart my haystack." Jason pretended to cry. "I

33

worked really hard on it, and now it's ruined! Waaaaaa!"

"Is that true, girls?" Ms. Frick asked, her ice-cream cone earrings swinging.

"Sort of," Nancy said slowly.

"Well," Ms. Frick said, "I suppose you'll have to build it again, won't you?"

Jason pumped his fist. "Yessss!"

"But . . . but . . ." Brenda said.

Nancy gave Brenda a look. "Yes, Ms. Frick," Brenda told the teacher.

"And don't be late for the bell," Ms. Frick warned. She headed toward the school. Jason ran after her.

"Ms. Frick," Nancy heard him call. Then he started to tell her about his Power Pumpkin idea.

"The haystack was all your idea, Nancy," Brenda snapped, grabbing bundles of hay. "Some detective you are."

Nancy glared back. Maybe helping Brenda was a big mistake.

The two girls put the haystack back together as fast as they could. Nancy was picking up the last bit of hay when she found something near the edge of the float. Cheery Charlie's spring glasses!

This is a clue, Nancy thought. She slipped them into her pocket.

Nancy tossed the hay onto the stack. She and Brenda ran into school just as the bell rang.

Nancy saw Bess and George walking down the hall to Mrs. Reynolds' class.

"Hi, Bess. Hi, George," Nancy called as she hurried to join them.

Bess frowned at Nancy. "You spent a long time out there with Brenda."

"What were you doing?" George asked. "Taking *princess* lessons?"

Nancy took a deep breath. "I . . . I can't really tell you," she said.

"What do you mean?" Bess said. "Best friends never keep secrets from each other."

George tossed her dark curls. "Maybe Nancy has a *new* best friend."

Nancy shook her head. But Bess and

35

George ran ahead to catch up with Jennifer.

"Tonight's my cousin's costume party," Nancy heard Jennifer say. "And I'm going to eat three slices of my aunt's cherry pie."

Then Nancy felt someone shake her shoulder.

"Look at Bess's knapsack," Brenda hissed. "There's something orange sticking out of it."

"So?" Nancy asked.

"It's got to be the cape from the Pumpkin Princess dress," Brenda insisted.

Nancy watched Bess stuff the knapsack into her cubby and walk into the classroom.

"I told you," Nancy said, "Bess isn't a suspect."

Brenda charged over to Bess's cubby.

"Don't you dare go through Bess's things, Brenda," Nancy whispered, following her.

It was too late. Brenda had tugged the orange fabric from Bess's knapsack.

She held up the cloth and scowled. It was a bright orange scarf.

"Phooey!" Brenda hurled it onto the floor.

Nancy picked up the scarf and started to stuff it back into Bess's knapsack. As she struggled with the zipper, a dark shadow slowly fell over her.

"Uh-oh." Nancy peered over her shoulder. Standing behind her—and looking very mad—was Bess!

5

The Dress Turns Up

H-hi, Bess," Nancy said.

"You and Brenda were going through my stuff, weren't you?" Bess said. She sounded really angry.

"I'm sorry, Bess," Nancy said. "I'll explain everything. One of these days."

"Don't bother," Bess told Nancy. Her long blond hair flipped out behind her as she turned to go into the classroom.

"Bess, wait!" Nancy cried.

"Let her go," Brenda said. "Who needs her anyway?"

Nancy faced Brenda. "I do! Bess was my best friend. She still would be if you hadn't made me keep this stupid secret!"

Brenda stuck out her chin. "You can't talk to me like that. I'm still the Pumpkin Princess!"

Nancy shook her head. "You don't even deserve to be princess, Brenda Carlton."

Suddenly, their teacher, Mrs. Reynolds, appeared at the classroom door. "Nancy, Brenda, class is about to start."

Nancy walked into the classroom.

I don't care if Brenda ever finds the dress, Nancy thought. Ever!

That evening Nancy tried to call Bess. But Bess wouldn't come to the phone.

What if she never speaks to me again? Nancy wondered as she hung up. She lifted the receiver and dialed George's number.

"George, I'm so glad you're home," Nancy said when George answered.

"Why were you going through Bess's cubby?" George asked. "She told me all about it."

Nancy was just about to tell George everything when she remembered the pinkie promise. Nancy didn't like it, but she was stuck helping Brenda.

"I can't explain now, but I will soon," Nancy said.

"You and Brenda have a secret together," George said.

Nancy didn't answer.

"That's what I thought," George said. "Bess is right not to talk to you."

"But, George," Nancy said, "what about Friends Till the End?"

"Maybe this *is* the end," George said. Then she hung up.

Later, at dinner, Nancy was so sad she didn't even feel like talking to her father.

"Pudding Pie, you're hardly eating Hannah's cherry cheesecake," Carson Drew said during dessert.

"Oh, Daddy," Nancy said, "I'm just not very hungry." She spilled a drop of cherry sauce on her white sweater.

"What's bothering you, Nancy?" her

40

father asked, dabbing Nancy's stain with a napkin.

Carson Drew was a lawyer and often helped Nancy with her mysteries. But today Nancy needed help with her friends.

"Well, I promised Brenda I would keep a secret for her," Nancy said. "Now Bess and George are mad at me because I can't tell them."

"Sounds serious," Mr. Drew said.

Nancy hung her head. Her father lifted her chin with his hand.

"Don't worry, Pudding Pie," he said. "If Bess and George are really your friends, they'll come around."

The next morning Nancy was awakened by Hannah knocking on her bedroom door.

"Oh, Sleeping Beauty," Hannah called. "There's someone here to see you."

Nancy rolled out of bed.

Maybe it's Bess or George, she thought, running down the stairs.

"Good morning, Detective Drew," Brenda called from the bottom of the staircase.

"Brenda," Nancy said, disappointed. "What do you want?"

"Don't tell me you forgot!" Brenda cried. "The dress rehearsal is this afternoon. We have to find my dress this morning, or else!"

"But, Brenda—"

"My bike is outside," Brenda said. "While you get dressed, I'll wait in the kitchen. I smell pancakes."

Nancy trudged up the stairs. The last thing she wanted to do was help Brenda. But she had promised to solve the mystery.

Nancy sighed. "And a promise is a promise."

After dressing, Nancy ate a quick breakfast. Then she headed outside with Brenda.

"So what's next?" Brenda asked as they hopped on their bikes.

Nancy pulled the spring eyeglasses

from her pants pocket. "I want to ask Cheery Charlie about these glasses. I found them on the float yesterday."

Nancy and Brenda rode down Main Street. Nancy slowed down when she saw Cheery Charlie's Costume and Joke Shop at the next corner.

"Why are we slowing down?" Brenda asked.

Nancy stopped her bike and pointed. Mrs. Marvin was coming out of Cheery Charlie's store.

"Look at all that money she's got," Brenda whispered.

Sure enough, Mrs. Marvin was smiling and counting a wad of bills.

"That's it!" Brenda said. "Bess stole the dress, and now Mrs. Marvin sold it to Creepy Charlie."

"It's *Cheery* Charlie," Nancy said. "And *he's* a suspect, not Bess."

"I say we go inside and make him confess," Brenda said. "We'll put on those hand buzzers he sells and shake both his hands until he talks."

44

"No," Nancy said. "We'll go inside and ask him nicely."

Nancy and Brenda waited until Mrs. Marvin was out of sight. They parked their bikes and entered Cheery Charlie's shop.

Charlie was near the counter. He was demonstrating a whoopee cushion to a group of customers.

"It's a good thing he's busy." Brenda grabbed Nancy's arm. "Now we can search the store."

Nancy and Brenda walked through the shop. Brenda is so pushy, Nancy thought. She picked up a rubber spider and dangled it over Brenda's head.

"Eeewwww!" Brenda quickly put a hand over her mouth.

Nancy giggled.

Soon the girls found an open door in the back of the shop. It had a sign on it that said Employees Only. "That's probably the storage room," Nancy said.

"Well? What are we waiting for?" Brenda asked, going through the door.

Nancy ran in after her.

Then the two girls froze. Their mouths were open.

Draped on a dressmaker's dummy in the middle of the room was the Pumpkin Princess dress!

6

Barnyard Bandits

Look what he did to my beautiful dress!" Brenda wailed. "It's ruined!"

Nancy stared at the Pumpkin Princess dress. The cape and sequins were gone, and it was stuck with a million pins.

"I'm taking it home right now," Brenda said, tugging at the dress.

Nancy heard the sound of footsteps. "Someone's coming," she whispered.

Brenda stopped. "What do we do?"

"We have to hide." Nancy looked around the room. Masks hung on the walls and from the ceiling. Dummies were everywhere, dressed in all sorts of costumes.

Brenda pointed to a nearby door.

"Let's hide in there!" she said.

Nancy and Brenda ran to the door. Brenda put her hand on the knob and pulled.

"EEEEEEEK!!"

"AAAAAAAHHHH!"

Dozens of rubber worms poured out and slithered down their heads.

"What are you doing in my supply closet?" Cheery Charlie demanded.

Nancy shook a heap of worms from her hair.

Brenda spit a worm from her mouth and pointed to the orange dress. "I want my dress back!"

Charlie scratched his chin. "That can't be yours."

"Why not?" Brenda asked.

"Because Mrs. Marvin just started sewing it today," Cheery Charlie said.

"You mean she's sewing *another* Pumpkin Princess dress?" Nancy asked.

Charlie nodded. "After I saw the dress at your school the other day, I

asked Mrs. Marvin to make one just like it for my store."

Charlie gave the girls a cheery grin. "If ya can't lick 'em, join 'em!"

"But what about your other pumpkin costume?" Nancy asked.

Charlie waved his hand in disgust. "Save it for Peter Peter Pumpkin Eater." He pointed to the princess dress. "Soon every girl in River Heights will get to be a Pumpkin Princess."

Brenda put her hands on her hips. "There's only one Pumpkin Princess in this town, mister—me!"

Nancy took Brenda aside. "At least we know he didn't steal the dress," she whispered.

Then she turned to Cheery Charlie. "I found something on our float yesterday that might belong to you, Charlie."

She reached into her pants pocket and pulled out the spring eyeglasses.

"I was wondering where I'd lost those," Charlie said, taking the glasses.

Nancy and Brenda turned to leave, but Charlie stopped them. "Wait. You were so honest to return my glasses. May I offer you something from my shop?"

Brenda ran straight to a glittery mermaid costume. But Nancy's eyes fell on some animal suits in the back of the room.

I know, Nancy thought. If Brenda and I dress up as animals, we could check out the River Street kids at their barnyard float.

"Is it okay if we borrow the sheep and the cow costumes?" Nancy asked Cheery Charlie.

Charlie nodded.

"What?" Brenda shrieked.

Nancy smiled at Brenda. "Don't worry. I know what I'm doing."

Nancy and Brenda parked their bikes in front of River Street Elementary School.

"I feel like a jerk!" Brenda said, straightening her cow mask. *"Beef jerky!"*

"I told you, Brenda," Nancy said. "If

the River Street kids stole the dress, they probably stashed it near their float."

"Why?" Brenda asked.

"Because they were wearing their animal costumes the day they were spying on us," Nancy explained. "They had to have gone back to the float."

"So now *we're* going to spy on *them?*" Brenda asked.

Nancy adjusted her fluffy sheep costume. "Let's just say we're going to pull the wool over their eyes."

"Cute." Brenda smirked.

Nancy and Brenda walked into the River Street schoolyard. They slipped into the crowd of kids in animal costumes.

"There's the float," Brenda said, pointing.

Nancy looked at the small red barn set on top of a platform. It had a white fence around it. Fake grass and hay were scattered across the floor. "I still like our float better," she said.

A teacher blew a whistle for attention. "Okay, kids!" he called out. "Take your places for the Old MacDonald dance."

"Nancy," Brenda whispered. "We don't know the steps."

"We'll pretend," Nancy said.

Nancy and Brenda followed the kids as they took their places around the float.

"Okay!" the teacher called out. "When the music starts, I want to see some fancy hoofin'!"

Soon the tune of "Old MacDonald's Farm" could be heard throughout the schoolyard.

Nancy watched the kids spin and kick up their heels. She and Brenda tried to copy them, but the River Street kids were going too fast.

"Nancy!" Brenda cried. "I can't—"

"Yes, you can!" Nancy cried back.

But it was no use. Brenda stepped on her tail and tumbled to the ground. Nancy tripped over Brenda and landed on top of her in a heap.

The teacher turned off the music. "I

don't remember having a sheep and a cow in this number," he said.

Then a boy in a moose costume marched over to Nancy and Brenda. He reached down and yanked the masks off their heads.

"That's because they're Carl Sandburg spies!"

7

Ms. Frick Sees Red

Great," Nancy muttered as the Barnyard Brigade surrounded her and Brenda.

Then she stood up and faced the crowd. "Something was stolen from our float. We think it's around here somewhere."

The River Street kids mumbled to one another.

"Is that true?" the teacher asked the kids. "Did someone take something from the Carl Sandburg float?"

Nobody answered.

"If no one speaks up, I'll cancel our part in the parade," the teacher warned.

A boy in a pig costume was shoved forward. "Okay, okay," he said. "I did borrow something from their float."

"*Borrow?*" Nancy asked.

Brenda ran over to the boy. "I bet it was orange," she said.

"Yeah, it's orange, all right." He pointed to the barn set on top of their float. "And it's in there."

Nancy and Brenda climbed onto the float. Now they could see inside the barn. Grinning at them was a large orange pumpkin head!

Brenda groaned. "It's only Jason's stupid pumped-up Power Pumpkin."

"When did you take this?" Nancy asked the boy in the pig costume.

"Early this morning," the boy admitted. He pointed to the rooster and the moose. "They dared me to."

Brenda held the pumpkin head out to the boys. "Here, keep it."

"No," Nancy told Brenda. "It belongs to us."

As Nancy and Brenda turned to leave, someone shouted out, "Only

dweebs go to Carl Sandburg Elementary School!"

Nancy whirled around. It was the boy in the moose costume.

A girl dressed as a duck charged over to the moose boy. "You take that back. My cousin Jennifer goes to Carl Sandburg!"

"Apologize to Tracy and the other girls, Gary," the teacher ordered.

Gary mumbled an apology and stormed off.

"Excuse me," Nancy said to Tracy. "But what's your cousin's name?"

"Jennifer Young," Tracy answered.

"Then you must be the one who gave the costume party last night," Nancy said.

Tracy nodded. "It was fun. And you should have seen Jennifer. Her costume was totally awesome! I've never seen a dress so beautiful."

That's strange, Nancy said to herself. I thought Jennifer was going to wear her old gypsy costume to the party.

After returning the cow and sheep

outfits to Cheery Charlie, Nancy and Brenda rode their bikes to the Carl Sandburg schoolyard.

"So far we've ruled out Cheery Charlie and the Barnyard Brigade," Nancy called over to Brenda. "I'll have to cross their names out of my notebook."

"I still say that Bess took the dress," Brenda said as she and Nancy pedaled to their school.

"I still say no," Nancy said.

"Then who did it?" Brenda asked.

Nancy glanced at the pumpkin head in her bicycle basket. "It could still be Jason. Just because he didn't bury the dress in the haystack doesn't mean he didn't hide it somewhere else."

Suddenly Bess's bike pulled up alongside them.

"Hi, Bess!" Nancy called out.

"Shhhh!" Brenda warned Nancy. "Don't say a single word to her!"

Nancy watched a hurt expression come over Bess's face.

"It's not what you think, Bess!"

Nancy tried to tell her. But Bess was already pedaling way ahead of them.

When Nancy and Brenda parked their bikes in the schoolyard, Jason ran over.

"So that's where my pumpkin head was," Jason shouted. "You stole it!"

Brenda flashed an angry look at Jason. "How dare you accuse Nancy of stealing when you probably stole the Pumpkin Princess dress."

"What are you talking about?" Jason asked. "The princess dress is in the gym right now."

Nancy and Brenda dashed into the gym. The orange velvet cape was on the rack. The princess dress was hanging next to it. But it was covered with red stains!

"What a mess," Ms. Frick was saying as she looked at the dress.

"What happened?" Nancy gasped.

"I found the dress and the cape stuffed in a plastic bag this morning," Ms. Frick said. She turned to Brenda. "Did you take them home, Brenda?"

"No, Ms. Frick," Brenda said.

"She really didn't," Nancy agreed. "I know for sure."

"How, Nancy?" Ms. Frick asked.

Nancy's mouth felt as dry as cotton. "I . . . I . . . just know," she said.

Ms. Frick shook her head. "I'm afraid that's not good enough, Nancy."

"Does this mean I can't be the Pumpkin Princess?" Brenda asked.

"No one will be princess until I get to the bottom of this," Ms. Frick said.

From the look on Brenda's face, Nancy thought she was about to cry.

"Nancy, hurry and put on your corn costume," Ms. Frick said.

She called to Jason, who was watching from the back of the gym. "Jason, get your Power Pumpkin mask ready. You might have to take the throne."

"All right!" Jason shouted happily.

"That's not fair," Brenda complained.

Ms. Frick examined the dress. "I'll have to call Mrs. Marvin for help," she said, and left the gym.

Nancy started pulling on her costume over her clothes.

"Well, at least the dress turned up," Nancy told Brenda.

"A lot of good that does me!" Brenda snapped, and walked away.

When Nancy had her corn costume on, she studied the princess dress carefully. The stains looked familiar. Sort of like the cherry sauce from Hannah's cheesecake.

Wait a minute, Nancy said to herself. Jennifer had planned to eat cherry pie at her cousin Tracy's party.

Then Nancy thought of something else. Jennifer hadn't wanted to wear her gypsy dress because Tracy had already seen it. But Tracy said that she'd never seen such a beautiful dress before.

"Okay," Nancy said under her breath. "Jennifer ate cherry pie last night. And she didn't wear her old costume." She began to pace back and forth. "If Jennifer took the princess dress, it had to be after Brenda put it on the float. And before Brenda went back for it."

Nancy's eyes opened wide. There was only one other clue that could prove Jennifer took the costume: George's cast.

Everyone had signed George's cast, even Brenda. If Jennifer's name was on it, then she couldn't have sneaked back to the float to steal the dress. But if she hadn't signed the cast . . .

Nancy dashed out of the gym and into the schoolyard. She ran straight to Bess.

"Bess, where's George?" Nancy asked.

"Why do *you* want to know?" Bess asked coolly. She was already dressed in her broccoli costume.

"Because I need to see her cast," Nancy pleaded.

"Well, you'd better see it soon." Bess put her hands on her hips. "Because George is probably getting it cut off right now!"

8

The Parade Marches On

But George just got her new cast two days ago," Nancy said to Bess. She had a sinking feeling in her stomach.

"One of her neighbors dropped a goldfish down it," Bess explained. "It was really starting to stink."

"Oh," Nancy said.

"Why should you care, anyway?" Bess asked. She began to walk away.

"Bess!" Nancy cried. "Isn't George's doctor right near here?"

Bess nodded. "His name is Dr. Cutler."

"Come with me while I speak to George," Nancy pleaded.

"Why should I?" Bess asked.

"George probably won't talk to me unless you're there," Nancy explained. "And this is very important."

Bess tilted her head. "How important?"

"There's not enough time to explain," Nancy said. "But it has something to do with our float."

Bess's eyes opened wide. "Our float? Then it must be important!"

"Will you come with me?" Nancy asked.

Bess stared down at her costume. "But we're dressed like dopey vegetables!"

"Come on." Nancy pulled Bess's arm. "Nobody will notice."

"I ordered a pizza, not vegetables," the nurse said when Nancy and Bess ran into Dr. Cutler's office.

Nancy tried to catch her breath. "I have to see George Fayne. Where is she, please?"

The nurse nodded toward a door. "She's in there, but—"

"Thank you," Nancy said. She ran to the door and pushed it open. Dr. Cutler was standing next to George with a tiny electric saw in his hand.

"Stop!" Nancy shouted, waving her arms.

"Nancy? Bess?" George said.

"Dr. Cutler," Nancy said. "I have to read the names on George's cast before you cut it off."

"Be my guest." The doctor smiled at Nancy. "Just remember, I wouldn't do this for junk food."

Nancy ran over to George. She began reading the names one by one: "Ms. Frick, Jason, Tim, Karen—"

"*Princess* Brenda." Bess rolled her eyes.

"Don't forget the back." George sighed, lifting her arm.

"Todd, Amy, Ryan, Tiffany, and us," Nancy read. "Just as I thought. Jennifer Young did not sign this cast."

"Now may I cut it off?" Dr. Cutler asked, holding up his saw.

"Oh, sure," Nancy said.

The doctor pushed a switch.

WHHHHHHHIIIIIIIRRRRRRRRRRRR!

*   *   *

As they walked back to school, Nancy filled Bess in on everything.

"Now do you see why I couldn't tell you or George?" Nancy asked.

"I guess," Bess said. "But I'm still not happy that you kept a secret from us. We could have helped you, Nancy."

Nancy nodded. "I know. But there's something you can help me with now."

"What?" Bess asked.

"You can help me talk to Jennifer."

At first Nancy and Bess couldn't find Jennifer. Instead they saw Brenda leaning against a tree and looking sad.

"There's Jennifer," Bess said.

Jennifer was behind the tree, struggling to sit down in her pea pod costume.

"Hi, Nancy. Hi, Bess," Jennifer said. "After this I don't think I'll ever eat peas again."

Nancy got right to the point.

"I met your cousin Tracy this morning," she said. "She told me you wore an awesome dress to her party."

Jennifer stared at Nancy. "She did?"

Brenda poked her head around the tree. "She did?"

"You said you were going to wear an old gypsy costume," Bess said.

Jennifer's eyes flashed. "I did. I just tied a few ribbons and bows on it. I looked practically like . . . a princess."

"You mean a Pumpkin Princess," Nancy said.

Brenda marched up to Jennifer. "How could you steal my dress, you little sneak?" she shouted.

"I didn't steal it!" Jennifer shouted back. "And I'm not a sneak!"

Ms. Frick and Mrs. Marvin walked over. "What's going on, girls?" Ms. Frick asked.

Brenda pointed to Jennifer. "She took the princess dress home, Ms. Frick. Ask her yourself."

"Jennifer?" Mrs. Marvin asked. "Is that true?"

Jennifer's eyes filled with tears. "I only wanted to borrow the dress for the costume party. I didn't think I'd drip cherry sauce all over it."

"What you did was wrong, Jennifer," Ms. Frick said.

"I didn't think so at the time," Jennifer admitted. "Brenda was being such a pain."

Nancy could see Brenda turn red.

Jennifer turned to Ms. Frick and Mrs. Marvin. "I'm sorry I took the dress home. I'll do anything to make up for it."

Mrs. Marvin stepped forward. "I have an idea, Jennifer. Can you sew?"

Sunday was a perfect day for a parade. Hundreds of people cheered as the colorful floats glided down Main Street.

The Pumpkin Patch Dream float was pulled by Ms. Frick's Jeep. It was right behind a real-live marching band.

"We make a great bunch of veggies!" Nancy shouted in her bright yellow corn costume.

"Like peas in a pod!" Jennifer yelled back.

Nancy could see Jason on his haystack while Brenda waved from her tree stump throne.

The princess dress looked beautiful. The sequins sparkled in the sunlight. Jennifer and Mrs. Marvin had done a great job sewing patches in the shape of fall leaves all over the skirt to cover the stains.

"I'm glad we still have a Pumpkin Princess," Nancy told Bess.

Bess nodded. "Even if it *is* Brenda."

"Everyone in River Heights must be here today." Nancy looked at the crowd of people and smiled.

Just then Nancy spotted George. She was cheering and waving a copy of the *Carlton News* with her good hand.

"Read it, Nan!" George shouted.

Nancy squinted and read the front page. In bold black ink it said: "Nancy Drew Is the World's Greatest Detective!"

Nancy looked up at the tree stump throne. Brenda shrugged. Nancy had kept her part of the promise, so Brenda had kept hers.

"Friends till the end?" Bess whispered in Nancy's ear.

"Friends till the end!" Nancy said happily.

That night Nancy had many reasons to be glad. The Pumpkin Patch Dream float won first prize. But best of all, Nancy, Bess, and George were best friends again.

Nancy pulled out her special blue notebook and started to write:

I learned a lot from this case. First, how important it is to keep a promise, no matter how hard it is. Second, being a good detective means using your skills to help people—even if the person you help is someone you don't really like.

Nancy tapped the pencil on her chin and wrote something else:

And being called the Greatest Detective in the World doesn't hurt, either!
Case closed.

NANCY DREW® MYSTERY STORIES By Carolyn Keene

☐ #58: THE FLYING SAUCER MYSTERY	72320-0/$3.99	
☐ #62: THE KACHINA DOLL MYSTERY	67220-7/$3.99	
☐ #68: THE ELUSIVE HEIRESS	62478-4/$3.99	
☐ #72: THE HAUNTED CAROUSEL	66227-9/$3.99	
☐ #73: ENEMY MATCH	64283-9/$3.50	
☐ #77: THE BLUEBEARD ROOM	66857-9/$3.50	
☐ #79: THE DOUBLE HORROR OF FENLEY PLACE	64387-8/$3.99	
☐ #81: MARDI GRAS MYSTERY	64961-2/$3.99	
☐ #83: THE CASE OF THE VANISHING VEIL	63413-5/$3.99	
☐ #84: THE JOKER'S REVENGE	63414-3/$3.99	
☐ #85: THE SECRET OF SHADY GLEN	63416-X/$3.99	
☐ #87: THE CASE OF THE RISING STAR	66312-7/$3.99	
☐ #89: THE CASE OF THE DISAPPEARING DEEJAY	66314-3/$3.99	
☐ #91: THE GIRL WHO COULDN'T REMEMBER	66316-X/$3.99	
☐ #92: THE GHOST OF CRAVEN COVE	66317-8/$3.99	
☐ #93: THE CASE OF THE SAFECRACKER'S SECRET	66318-6/$3.99	
☐ #94: THE PICTURE-PERFECT MYSTERY	66319-4/$3.99	
☐ #96: THE CASE OF THE PHOTO FINISH	69281-X/$3.99	
☐ #97: THE MYSTERY AT MAGNOLIA MANSION	69282-8/$3.99	
☐ #98: THE HAUNTING OF HORSE ISAND	69284-4/$3.99	
☐ #99: THE SECRET AT SEVEN ROCKS	69285-2/$3.99	
☐ #101: THE MYSTERY OF THE MISSING MILLIONAIRES	69287-9/$3.99	
☐ #102: THE SECRET IN THE DARK	69279-8/$3.99	
☐ #104: THE MYSTERY OF THE JADE TIGER	73050-9/$3.99	
☐ #107: THE LEGEND OF MINER'S CREEK	73053-3/$3.99	
☐ #109: THE MYSTERY OF THE MASKED RIDER	73055-X/$3.99	
☐ #110: THE NUTCRACKER BALLET MYSTERY	73056-8/$3.99	
☐ #111: THE SECRET AT SOLAIRE	79297-0/$3.99	
☐ #112: CRIME IN THE QUEEN'S COURT	79298-9/$3.99	
☐ #113: THE SECRET LOST AT SEA	79299-7/$3.99	
☐ #114: THE SEARCH FOR THE SILVER PERSIAN	79300-4/$3.99	
☐ #115: THE SUSPECT IN THE SMOKE	79301-2/$3.99	
☐ #116: THE CASE OF THE TWIN TEDDY BEARS	79302-0/$3.99	
☐ #117: MYSTERY ON THE MENU	79303-9/$3.99	
☐ #118: TROUBLE AT LAKE TAHOE	79304-7/$3.99	
☐ #119: THE MYSTERY OF THE MISSING MASCOT	87202-8/$3.99	
☐ #120: THE CASE OF THE FLOATING CRIME	87203-6/$3.99	
☐ #121: THE FORTUNE-TELLER'S SECRET	87204-4/$3.99	
☐ #122: THE MESSAGE IN THE HAUNTED MANSION	87205-2/$3.99	
☐ #123: THE CLUE ON THE SILVER SCREEN	87206-0/$3.99	
☐ #124: THE SECRET OF THE SCARLET HAND	87207-9/$3.99	
☐ #125: THE TEEN MODEL MYSTERY	87208-7/$3.99	
☐ #126: THE RIDDLE IN THE RARE BOOK	87209-5/$3.99	
☐ #127: THE CASE OF THE DANGEROUS SOLUTION	50500-9/$3.99	
☐ #128: THE TREASURE IN THE ROYAL TOWER	50502-5/$3.99	
☐ #129: THE BABYSITTER BURGLARIES	50507-6/$3.99	
☐ #130: THE SIGN OF THE FALCON	50508-4/$3.99	
☐ #131: THE HIDDEN INHERITANCE	50509-2/$3.99	
☐ #132: THE FOX HUNT MYSTERY	50510-6/$3.99	
☐ #133: THE MYSTERY AT THE CRYSTAL PALACE	50515-7/$3.99	
☐ #134: THE SECRET OF THE FORGOTTEN CAVE	50516-5/$3.99	
☐ #135: THE RIDDLE OF THE RUBY GAZELLE	00048-9/$3.99	
☐ #136: THE WEDDING DAY MYSTERY	00050-0/$3.99	
☐ #137: IN SEARCH OF THE BLACK ROSE	00051-9/$3.99	
☐ #138: THE LEGEND OF THE LOST GOLD	00049-7/$3.99	
☐ NANCY DREW GHOST STORIES	69132-5/$3.99	
☐ #139: THE SECRET OF CANDLELIGHT INN	00052-7/$3.99	
☐ #140: THE DOOR-TO-DOOR DECEPTION	00053-5/$3.99	
☐ #141: THE WILD CAT CRIME	00120-5/$3.99	
☐ #142: THE CASE OF CAPTIAL INTRIGUE	00751-3/$3.99	

A MINSTREL® BOOK

Published by Pocket Books

THE HARDY BOYS® SERIES By Franklin W. Dixon

FULL HOUSE™ Michelle

#5: THE GHOST IN MY CLOSET 53573-0/$3.99

#6: BALLET SURPRISE 53574-9/$3.99

#7: MAJOR LEAGUE TROUBLE 53575-7/$3.99

#8: MY FOURTH-GRADE MESS 53576-5/$3.99

#9: BUNK 3, TEDDY, AND ME 56834-5/$3.99

#10: MY BEST FRIEND IS A MOVIE STAR!
(Super Edition) 56835-3/$3.99

#11: THE BIG TURKEY ESCAPE 56836-1/$3.99

#12: THE SUBSTITUTE TEACHER 00364-X/$3.99

#13: CALLING ALL PLANETS 00365-8/$3.99

#14: I'VE GOT A SECRET 00366-6/$3.99

#15: HOW TO BE COOL 00833-1/$3.99

#16: THE NOT-SO-GREAT OUTDOORS 00835-8/$3.99

#17: MY HO-HO-HORRIBLE CHRISTMAS 00836-6/$3.99

MY AWESOME HOLIDAY FRIENDSHIP BOOK
(An Activity Book) 00840-4/$3.99

FULL HOUSE MICHELLE OMNIBUS 02181-8/$6.99

#18: MY ALMOST PERFECT PLAN 00837-4/$3.99

#19: APRIL FOOLS 01729-2/$3.99

A MINSTREL® BOOK
Published by Pocket Books

Simon & Schuster Mail Order Dept. BWB
200 Old Tappan Rd., Old Tappan, N.J. 07675

Please send me the books I have checked above. I am enclosing $_____ (please add $0.75 to cover the postage and handling for each order. Please add appropriate sales tax). Send check or money order--no cash or C.O.D.'s please. Allow up to six weeks for delivery. For purchase over $10.00 you may use VISA: card number, expiration date and customer signature must be included.

Name _____

Address _____

City _____ State/Zip _____

VISA Card # _____ Exp.Date _____

Signature _____

1033-26

**Do your younger brothers and sisters
want to read books like yours?**

**Let them know there
are books just for *them!***

They can join Nancy Drew and her best
friends as they collect clues and solve
mysteries in

THE
NANCY DREW
NOTEBOOKS®

Starting with
#1 The Slumber Party Secret
#2 The Lost Locket

AND

**Meet up with suspense and mystery
in Frank and Joe Hardy:
The Clues Brothers™**

#1 The Gross Ghost Mystery
#2 The Karate Clue

Look for a brand-new story every
other month at your local bookseller

A MINSTREL BOOK

Published by Pocket Books   1366-01